Dear Parent:
Your child's love of reading starts here!

I Can Read Books have introduced children to the joy of reading since 1957. Featuring award-winning authors and illustrators and a fabulous cast of beloved characters, I Can Read Books set the standard for beginning readers. From books your child reads with you to the first books they read alone, there are I Can Read Books for every stage of reading:

SHARED READING
Basic language, word repetition, and whimsical illustrations, ideal for sharing with your emergent reader

BEGINNING READING
Short sentences, familiar words, and simple concepts for children eager to read on their own

READING WITH HELP
Engaging stories, longer sentences, and language play for developing readers

READING ALONE
Complex plots, challenging vocabulary, and high-interest topics for the independent reader

ADVANCED READING
Short paragraphs, chapters, and exciting themes for the perfect bridge to chapter books

Every child learns in a different way and at their own speed. Some read through each level in order. Others go back and forth between levels and read favorite books again and again. You can help your young reader improve and become more confident by encouraging their own interests and abilities.

A lifetime of discovery begins with the magical words, **"I Can Read!"**

To Katherine Tegen and Julie Hittman,
our fairy godmothers

Pish and Posh Text copyright © 2004 by Barbara Bottner and Gerald Kruglik Illustrations copyright © 2004 by Barbara Bottner
All rights reserved. No part of this book may be used or reproduced in any manner whatsoever without written permission except
in the case of brief quotations embodied in critical articles and reviews. Printed in the United States of America. For information
address HarperCollins Children's Books, a division of HarperCollins Publishers, 1350 Avenue of the Americas, New York,
NY 10019. www.harperchildrens.com

Library of Congress Cataloging-in-Publication Data
Bottner, Barbara. Pish and Posh / by Barbara Bottner and Gerald Kruglik ; pictures by Barbara Bottner.—1st ed.   p.   cm. —
(An I can read book) Summary: When Pish and Posh discover fairy magic, they face a series of wacky surprises.
ISBN 0-06-051416-7 — ISBN 0-06-051417-5 (lib. bdg.) — ISBN 0-06-051418-3 (pbk.) [1. Fairies—Fiction.
2. Magic—Fiction. 3. Lost and found possessions.—Fiction.] I. Kruglik, Gerald. II. Title. III. Series.
PZ7.B6586Pi 2004 [E]—dc21   2003001870

❖

An I Can Read Book™

Pish and Posh

by Barbara Bottner
and Gerald Kruglik

pictures by Barbara Bottner

KATHERINE TEGEN BOOKS
An Imprint of HarperCollins*Publishers*

After dinner, there was a loud *thud*

outside the front door.

"Pish!" yelled Posh,

Pish's very best friend,

"Someone left us a present!

The Fairy Handbook!"

"We are not becoming fairies,"
said Pish,
after she finished her pudding.
"I think becoming a fairy
is a *good* idea," said Posh.
"Most of your ideas turn out
to be very *bad* ideas," said Pish.

"Anyway, you have to finish the dishes.

I am going to work on my puzzle."

Posh wondered if a fairy

could clean up a sink

faster than she could.

She flipped open the book.

Chapter One was

How to Clean Dirty Dishes.

Posh thought about how Pish liked

to read books from the beginning.

But she was Posh, not Pish.

The book read,

"Just clap, sing the second line

of your favorite song,

jump backward, and. . . ."

Posh got the idea.

She clapped, sang the second line

of "Yankee Doodle"

(or was it the third line?),

and jumped.

Nothing happened.

"Are you finished?" asked Pish,

who was always getting

things done.

Posh went back outside to practice.

On the steps now sat a shining wand.

She grabbed the wand

and ran in to the sink.

The pile of dishes

looked even bigger than before.

Posh didn't have time

to read a long, boring chapter

about wands.

She waved the wand hard,

and it flew out of her hand

and hit the sink.

14

Water gushed from the faucet.

Soap poured over the sink.

Mountains of suds slid onto
the floor toward the living room.

"My puzzle is getting wet,"
called Pish.

"Well, doing the dishes
was a terrible idea!" said Posh.

"It was a *good* idea," said Pish,

"but the suds
need to *stay* in the sink."

Pish ran to the kitchen
and slipped on the soapy floor.

Posh laughed.

"Don't even speak to me," said Pish.

So Posh didn't speak to Pish.

Pish got up

and slammed

the faucet shut.

"There!" said Pish,

in that certain way that meant

she was pleased with herself.

"Have you been fooling

with that silly handbook?

Did you read the directions?"

asked Pish.

"It was a long chapter," said Posh.

How did Pish know everything?

Pish frowned.

"Why are you so frowny?" asked Posh.

"I am frowny because I fell.
I got wet. And I did not finish
my puzzle. Promise never, ever
to use *The Fairy Handbook* again."

Posh promised.

That night, Chapter Eight fell open.

It said, "Making Things Reappear."

This time Posh would read

all the directions.

She sat down to begin, but Pish yelled,

"Time for bed!"

The next morning, while Pish

finished her puzzle, Posh lay

in the hammock and watched the clouds.

Izzy, the boy next door, stopped by.

"My dog, Stan, is lost," he cried.

"I am learning fairy magic.

I can make him reappear," said Posh.

"He is small. He likes to swim

and hide under the bed," said Izzy.

Making things reappear was not easy.

Someone like Pish

could probably do it.

But she was only Posh.

Still, she had to try.

"First, leap on one foot

while holding your ear."

Which foot? Which ear?

Posh tried the left ear

and the left foot.

"Small!" she said.

Then she tried the right ear

and the right foot.

28

And the right ear with the left foot.

She almost fell down.

Finally, both feet, and both ears.

Nothing happened,

so Posh went inside.

The wand fell to the floor.

"You called?" said the smallest,

ugliest man Posh had ever seen.

"Who are you?" asked Posh.

"I'm the *smallest* of the small."

"Who are you talking to?"

called Pish.

"Nobody!" said Posh.

"I'm *not* a nobody," he said.

"I apologize," said Posh,

"but you're not Izzy's dog!

Now, would you mind hiding?"

Posh took the handbook

outside to think. This time,

a little packet called PIXIE DUST

slipped out. Posh leaped.

She raised the wand,

threw the dust into the air,

and yelled "Not so small!"

Nothing happened.

But back inside,

Posh faced the largest creature

she had ever seen.

She wondered if fairy magic

would ever make things *easier*

instead of harder.

"Mr. Giant, sir," she said,

"would you mind hiding in the closet?"

Stan liked to swim.

So Posh waved her wand

and threw pixie dust into the bathtub.

She called out "Swimming!"

"What am I doing here?"

asked a mermaid.

"I can't answer that right now,"

said Posh, "but would you mind

staying in the tub?"

Pish peeked around the corner.

"I smell the ocean," she said.

"No, you don't," said Posh.

What else did Izzy say

about his dog?

He loved to hide under the bed!

Posh touched her ear, sang,

and tossed lots of pixie dust

under the bed.

"You called?" came a voice

from the dark.

"No, not you!" said Posh.

"Nobody wants the Monster

Under the Bed,"

the voice said.

Pish went into the kitchen.

"Posh," called Pish, "when are you

going to clean up these dishes?"

Pish ran all over the house

looking for Posh.

"A mermaid? You promised

no more fairy magic!"

"But Izzy's dog is lost,"

Posh explained.

"Did you get him back?" asked Pish.

Posh shook her head.

"We better get started," said Pish,

who could sometimes be very nice.

Pish read Chapter Eight out loud.

"Think about Izzy's dog,"
Pish ordered Posh.

Posh thought very hard.

There was a knock on the door.

Pish and Posh opened it.

It was Izzy and Stan.

"Fairy magic works!" said Posh.

"Stan was not lost," said Izzy.

"He was in the park with my mother."

"Posh, take *The Fairy Handbook*,
this fairy wand, and this pixie dust
back outside," said Pish in a loud voice.
"Not yet!" called the monster,
the mermaid, the giant, and the troll.
"We want to go home!"

"Now, let's take care of this mess,"
said Pish, who read "How to Make
Things Return to Where They Belong"
from *The Fairy Handbook*.
There was quite a bit of work
to be done. Finally,
everyone disappeared.
The house was quiet again.
"Pish," said Posh, "being a fairy
is too much work. I quit!"
"Very wise, Posh," said Pish.
"But it's still your turn
to wash the dishes."

Posh scrubbed every pot and pan.

Pish returned *The Fairy Handbook*

outside, but did not go to bed

until it was quite late.